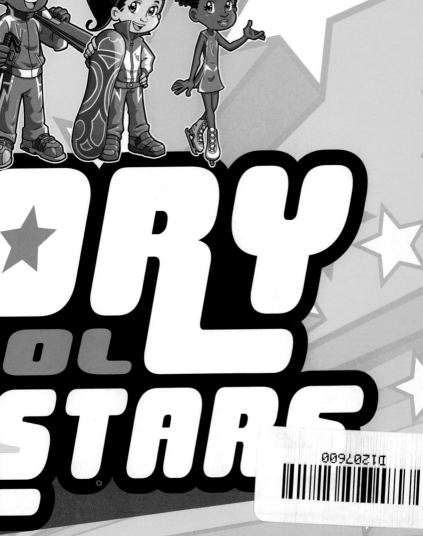

Skiing Has Its Ups and Downs

by **Scott Nickel**
illustrated by **Jorge Santillan**

STONE ARCH BOOKS
a capstone imprint

0.5pts.

VICTORY SCHOOL SUPERSTARS

Sports Illustrated KIDS *Skiing Has Its Ups and Downs*
is published by Stone Arch Books — A Capstone Imprint
151 Good Counsel Drive, P.O. Box 669
Mankato, Minnesota 56002
www.capstonepub.com

Art Director: Bob Lentz
Graphic Designer: Hilary Wacholz
Production Specialist: Michelle Biedscheid

Timeline photo credits: Shutterstock/Granite (top right),
Paul Cowan (top left); Sports Illustrated/Simon Bruty
(bottom left, middle, and bottom right).

Printed in the United States of America in Stevens Point, Wisconsin.
032011   006111WZF11

Library of Congress Cataloging-in-Publication Data
Nickel, Scott. Skiing has its ups and downs / by Scott Nickel; illustrated by
Jorge H. Santillan.
  p. cm. — (Sports Illustrated kids. Victory School superstars)
Summary: Danny wants to quit when he has difficulties learning how to
ski downhill.
ISBN 978-1-4342-2234-3 (library binding)
ISBN 978-1-4342-3395-0 (pbk.)
  1. Skis and skiing—Juvenile fiction. 2. Persistence—Juvenile fiction. [1.
Skis and skiing—Fiction. 2. Persistence—Fiction.] I. Santillan, Jorge, ill.
II. Title. III. Series: Sports Illustrated kids. Victory School superstars.
  PZ7.N557Sk 2011
  [Fic]—dc22   2011002309

TABLE OF CONTENTS

DANNY GOHL

AGE: 10
GRADE: 4
SUPER SPORTS ABILITY: Super Speed

Downhill Skiing

Triumph Mountain Superstars:

KENZIE

ALICIA

DANNY

TRIUMPH MOUNTAIN

Triumph Mountain is the leading sports-education resort in the country. It is home to dozens of ski lifts and a state-of-the-art ice arena and snowboard park. At Triumph, young athletes can learn their favorite winter sports from their favorite athletes.

1. Ice Arena
2. Lodge
3. Condos
4. Halfpipe
5. Jumps
6. Ski Slopes

Triumph Mountain

Whoosh!

I duck and feel the snowball whiz past my left ear.

Whoosh! Whoosh!

Two more zoom toward me. I twist my body and jerk my head to the right. Ha! Missed me again.

I zigzag in the snow, just like on the football field. Fake left. Fake right. More than a dozen snowballs come at me, but I'm too fast.

Just when I think the fight is over, I look up and see a huge mound of snow coming at me like a cannonball. I dive for the ground.

Splat! I turn and see my twin sister Alicia's snowball has hit someone else. And not just any someone, but Ace Faraday. He is a two-time gold medal winner and world record holder in downhill skiing.

Ace isn't just an Olympian. He's also my ski instructor here at Triumph Mountain Resort.

Every year, Victory School takes a special trip to introduce students to new sports. I had been looking forward to it for months, of course. But now I'll probably spend the whole trip in detention.

"Sorry, Coach Faraday!" I shout and rush over to him. He's sitting in the snow, his hair and chest covered by slush.

"Don't worry about it, Danny," he says. "Maybe you can bring those sharp reflexes — and your super speed — to the slopes."

I smile. "I hope so, Coach Faraday," I reply.

"I'll see you at practice in thirty minutes," Coach says, brushing snow from his shoulders. "Don't be late. Oh, and call me Ace."

"Sure thing, Ace!" I say.

I'm so excited about skiing lessons. On the bus ride to the resort, I sat with Josh, who's an expert on ice. All we could talk about was how cool this trip was.

We'd get to spend a whole week at Triumph Mountain Resort. We would get to try skiing, snowboarding, ice skating, and other winter sports. And who would be doing the teaching? Former Olympians, like Ace!

I know my speed will help me be the fastest downhill skier Triumph Mountain — and Ace Faraday — have ever seen.

CHAPTER 2

The First Lesson

At the morning lesson, Ace tells us about
our ski gear: boots, skis, poles, goggles,
helmet, and the most important of all —
bindings.

"The bindings hold your boots to the skis. We have to make sure that the bindings are set correctly," Ace warns. "You can get hurt if your skis don't release during a fall. But if the bindings release *too* easily, you'll be falling a lot more than normal."

Suiting up for skiing isn't like putting on a wrestling singlet or even a football jersey. With all those layers, I feel like I weigh a ton. I can barely move after I get everything on.

I'm used to pumping my legs like a machine to carry me across the field. Now my legs are wrapped up in big, clunky boots and strapped to a pair of long, flat sticks.

"I want us to have a good week,"
Ace says to the class. "I'm a friendly guy,
but I expect a lot from my students. Like
everything else, you get out of this sport
what you put in."

"Skiing isn't easy," Ace continues.
"It takes work, and it takes patience."

As a guy who does things fast, I don't
like to wait. "Forget patience," I say. "I
want to shred that hill!"

I push forward with my poles. But my skis get crossed, and I fall sideways onto the snow. *Oof!*

Alicia and Josh start laughing, and then all the other kids laugh, too. I even see Ace cover his mouth to hide a smile.

"You're going to fall a lot," Ace says, helping me up. "Don't worry about it. Before you know it, you'll be flying down the hill."

On the slopes, Ace goes over the basic moves. I try to focus on what he's saying, but all I want to do is fly down that hill.

"Hey, Alicia!" I shout. "Let's race!"

"Okay!" she says.

We push off, and I'm leaning forward, trying to get some speed. I twist my body and move my legs, but these moves mess with my balance. Still, I'm weaving down the slope.

When I look up, I see Alicia waiting at the bottom of the hill. She waves at me. My run takes forever, but I finally get to the bottom.

"Hey, Danny," Alicia says with a laugh, "want to race again?"

"Very funny," I say, gritting my teeth a little. I'm not used to coming in second, especially to my sister.

"I'll even give you a head start," Alicia says. She gives me a playful shove. "Who would ever believe that I beat Danny Gohl, the fastest kid at Victory School?"

"Ha-ha. Very funny," I say, looking away.

This is so embarrassing. And frustrating. I know I'm fast. So why am I so slow on the slopes?

Wipe Out!

That evening I can't enjoy my dinner. And I should, because it's my favorite — spaghetti with garlic bread.

"Aren't you hungry? I thought for sure you would need to eat after all that falling," Alicia jokes.

I slump down in my chair. It's going to be a long week.

The next day at practice isn't going much better than the first. I just can't seem to get the skis to do what I want them to do.

Ace sees my frustration. "You've got to work through it, Danny. Push yourself," he says.

"I will, Ace," I say. I don't want to let him down.

After class breaks up, I'm still in the mood to practice. I've got to get better. I want to show Ace that I have what it takes. I want to show myself, too.

I try a few runs down the slope. I get a little faster with each run, but it's still not enough.

Then something amazing happens. As I'm going downhill, something clicks. I get into a good rhythm. Ace calls it a groove. My body seems to have figured out what to do. I'm pushing myself, digging into the snow with my poles. I know I can do it.

I'm going faster and faster down the hill.
Uh-oh! Something's wrong. I'm moving too
fast. My legs wobble, and I hit a mound. I
feel my skis release from the bindings and
slide out from under me.

Then all I see is a white blur as I tumble down the hill. *Wipe out!*

For a second I'm not sure where I am. I hear someone calling my name. Alicia? Ace? Mom? My head feels kind of funny. Like when you spin around and around and can't keep your balance.

"Danny! Are you okay?" It's Alicia. She pulls me up. "Should we call ski patrol?" she asks.

"No, no," I protest. "I'm okay. I can walk."

Ace glides over to us. He looks directly into my eyes. "And that's why we wear helmets," he says. "Are you okay?"

I nod.

"Your eyes look good. If you feel sick or anything, be sure to let someone know."

"Sure thing," I say. "I guess I'll call it a day."

I try to smile. But it's the kind of smile you make when you're at the principal's office or the dentist. I don't think I fooled anyone.

CHAPTER 4

Tied in Knots

The next morning I'm still in bed when it's time for practice.

"Are you okay?" Josh asks.

"Um, it's my stomach," I say. "I think I'm going to have to skip ski practice today."

And it's not a lie. My stomach feels like it's all tied in knots.

"Okay," he says. "I'll tell Coach Faraday and let our chaperone know."

I know I'm letting Ace down, but I can't help it. Ever since the fall, my head has been buzzing with all kinds of thoughts. Maybe I was wrong to take on downhill skiing. What if I fall again? What if I get really hurt?

Maybe I should drop the class and switch to cross country skiing. I'd be able to use my legs more, and there's no danger of wiping out.

Ugh.

My stomach feels worse. I pull the covers over my head.

Rematch

That afternoon, I'm feeling a little better when Alicia, Josh, and a couple of kids from class stop by the condo.

"Ready for a rematch?" Alicia asks.

"Isn't class over?" I ask.

"Not in skiing. A snowball fight!" she yells.

Sounds good to me! I rush to put on my snow gear.

Outside, I'm using my speed to be a one-man snowball-making machine. "You're in for it now," I warn Alicia.

I feel a tap on my shoulder. It's Ace.

"Feeling better, I see," he says.

"I . . . um . . ." I'm busted.

"Don't worry about it," Ace says. "How about you take a break from the snowball fight and we talk?"

We start walking through the snow. The air is crisp, and the sun is out. It's a beautiful day.

"So when are we going to get you back on that hill, Danny?" Ace asks.

My stomach tightens again, but I manage to say, "Actually, Ace, I was thinking of switching to cross country."

Ace frowns. "I'd really hate to see you do that," he says. "You've got real skills. And your speed is a big asset."

"I thought it was. But if I go too fast, I could crash again," I say.

"Oh, you'll definitely crash! Skiing has its ups and downs," Ace says with a laugh. "That's part of the sport. I've fallen and crashed dozens of times. And a few of them were on TV in front of millions of people. How embarrassing is that?"

Ace puts his hand on my shoulder. "But I always got back up and on those skis. Sure, sometimes I was afraid. But fear is something you conquer. You don't let it conquer you."

I nod my head.

"Think about it, Danny," he says. "I hope to see you back on the hill at tomorrow's practice."

Running always helps me think, so I take off through the snow. The white stuff slows me down a little, but it feels good to have my legs pumping again. As I pass Alicia and the other kids, a snowball smashes into my face.

Splat!

I drop to the ground. Another snowball hits me. And then another.

For a second I'm dazed. Should I quit? Head back inside? No way! I think about what Coach said and shake the slush from my hair. I will not let a little fall conquer me!

I put on my gloves and start scooping up snow.

"Okay," I say with a laugh. "Let's finish this war!"

CHAPTER 6

Gaining Speed

The next morning, Ace gives me a grin as I gear up for practice.

At the top of the hill, I'm a little nervous. My stomach is tight again but I try to ignore it.

I wait for the other kids to make their runs. Alicia's gotten really good. She has excellent form and her speed is even better.

Finally, it's my turn.

I push off with my poles and start down the hill. I feel the crisp wind in my face, the smooth snow beneath me. Leaning forward, I'm ready for each turn, and I feel relaxed. I'm gaining speed — and confidence.

No matter what we do, we're eventually going to fall down. The trick is to always get back up, whether it's during a snowball fight or during a ski run. I'm glad now that Ace wouldn't let me take the easy way out.

I glide over a mound — my skis lifting off the snow — catching some air. The feeling is something I can't describe. I can't help shouting, "Wahoo!"

GLOSSARY

chaperone (SHAP-uh-rohn)—an adult who is responsible for the safety of young people at events

confidence (KON-fi-dens)—a strong belief in yourself

conquer (KONG-kur)—to defeat and take control

definitely (DEF-uh-nit-lee)—certainly

detention (di-TEN-shuhn)—a punishment in which a student has to stay after school

embarrassing (em-BARE-uss-ing)—something that makes you feel awkward and uncomfortable

frustrating (FRUHSS-trate-ing)—making someone feel helpless or discouraged

Olympian (oh-LIM-pee-an)—an athlete who competes in the Olympic games

patience (PAY-shuhnss)—ability to put up with problems or delays without getting angry or upset

reflexes (REE-flecks-es)—automatic actions that happen without a person's control or effort

DOWNHILL SKIING IN HISTORY

2500 B.C. People from Norway to Mongolia use wood and leather skis as transportation.

1849 A.C. U.S. mail carriers ski to far-off mining towns to deliver **mail**.

1868 Sondre Norheim of **Norway** uses stiff bindings that hold down his heel to win a skiing race.

1922 Arnold Lunn, an English travel agent, takes his clients on ski trips and creates downhill obstacle courses for them. This is called slalom skiing.

1936 Sun Valley resort in Idaho opens with the first chairlift.

1948 In St. Moritz, Switzerland, Gretchen Fraser is the first American to win a gold medal in an Olympic Alpine skiing event.

1952 The Olympics adds giant slalom as an event.

1998 Popular skier **Picabo Street** wins Olympic gold in super giant slalom

2008 Americans Lindsey Vonn and **Bode Miller** capture the overall World Cup titles.

2010 The **U.S. team** wins eight Alpine skiing medals at the Vancouver Olympics.

Danny Gohl Is Speeding Toward Victory!

If you liked *Danny's* adventure on the slopes, check out his other *sports stories*.

A Running Back Can't Always Rush

With his super speed, Danny can rush down the field in seconds. But when he forgets to slow down off the field, he faces big problems. How will Danny learn that a running back can't always rush?

It's a Wrestling Mat, Not a Dance Floor

With football season over, Danny tries wrestling. When he uses his super speed in his new sport, he ends up dancing all around. Danny's got to remember that it's a wrestling mat, not a dance floor.